MEET CHADWICK
AND HIS
CHESAPEAKE BAY FRIENDS

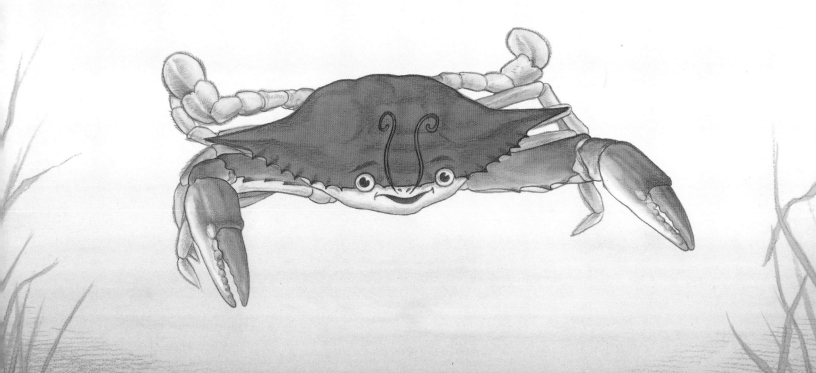

For William and Hannah
and their good friends
Sophie, Sam, and Shoogie
—P.C.

For Donna and Cynth
—A.R.C.

MEET CHADWICK
AND HIS
CHESAPEAKE BAY FRIENDS

By Priscilla Cummings

Illustrated by A.R.Cohen

Emily —
We wish you
many happy days
at the cottage
learning about
these animals.
Love,
Uncle Mike &
Aunt Cathy

For Emily —

Happy
Reading!

Priscilla
Cummings
2013

Schiffer ® Publishing Ltd

4880 Lower Valley Road • Atglen, PA 19310

If you would like to meet a crab,
A crab with googlie eyes,
Then come along and take a look.
You're in for a surprise!

Meet Chadwick, the Chesapeake Crab,
As happy as can be.
He lives beneath blue waters
In a bay, beside the sea.

He has eight legs to help him swim,
And two big pincers, too.
He swims and pinches all day long.
It's what crabs like to do!

Young Chadwick has a lot of friends
In the bay and on the beach.
Some like the water, some like land,
And some like some of each.

Some friends have noses, some have beaks,
And some of them have bills.
Some friends have feathers, some have fur,
And some of them have gills.

Meet Bernie, who's a sea gull,
Always looking for some lunch.
He loves a fish at dinnertime
And cookies by the bunch.

Friend Bernie is a fat old bird,
As happy as can be.
He eats his fish and flies above
The bay, beside the sea.

Meet Miss Matilda, white egret—
A proper one at that!
She always looks her very best
With flowers in her hat.

Matilda is a lady bird,
As fussy as can be.
She loves her mucky, muddy marsh
Near the bay, beside the sea.

Now meet Toulouse, the Canada Goose,
Who visits from the north.
He flies back home in spring and says
He likes the back and forth.

And hear Toulouse, the traveling goose,
Honk honking joyously.
He loves to spend his winters
At the bay, beside the sea.

Meet Hector Spector Jellyfish,
The silliest "fish" you'll find.
He goes this way, then that, because
He can't make up his mind!

Watch Hector Spector Jellyfish,
Wishy-washy as can be.
He doesn't know which way to go
In his bay, beside the sea.

Meet Belly Jeans the Flounder,
At the bottom of the bay.
He snuggles underneath the sand
And *there* he wants to stay!

See Belly Jeans the flounder fish,
As splat flat as can be.
He loves life at the bottom
Of the bay, beside the sea.

And now meet Orville Oyster, *shhh!*
It's hard to see his face.
He's very shy and quiet, too,
And stays in just *one* place!

His shell is hard and crusty,
And as solid as can be.
He calls that crusty shell his home
In the bay, beside the sea.

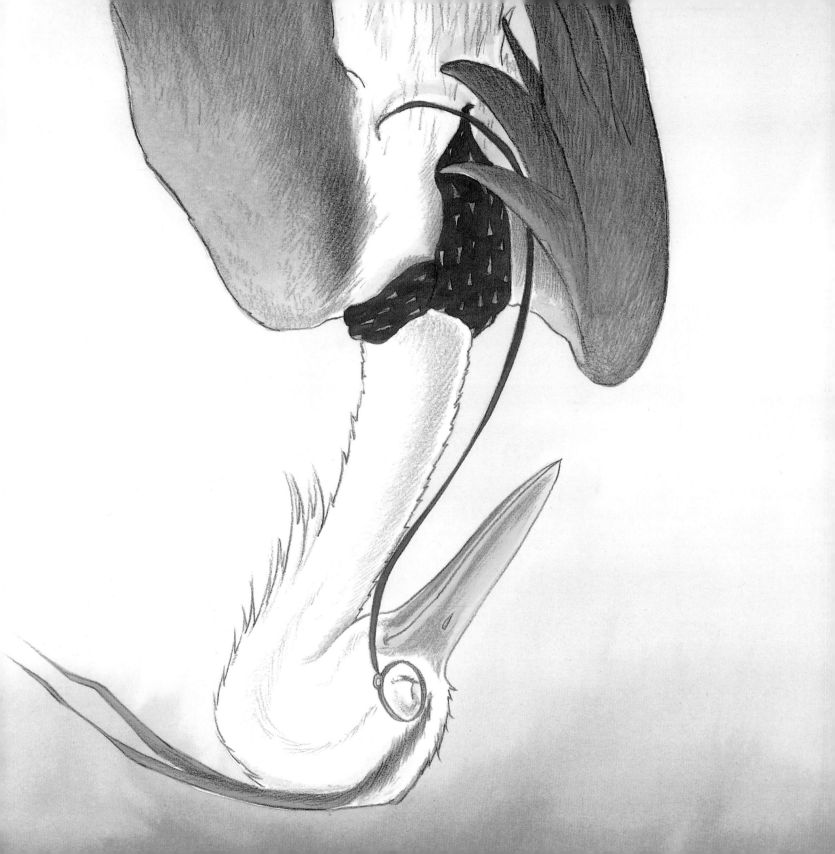

Meet stately Baron von Heron,
So tall and slim and blue.
He can be short when he wants to,
Or tall to see far, too.

The great blue Baron von Heron,
A bird of royalty.
He watches out for all his friends
In the bay, beside the sea.

Meet Sid and Sal, an osprey pair,
Who found a marker best
To build a home and spend their time
In a great big stick-filled nest.

They opened up a diner, too.
Friends eat there frequently.
The food is good at Sid and Sal's,
In the bay, beside the sea.

Meet Esmerelda, lady crab,
With claw tips all in red.
She loves cute Chadwick; he loves her.
That's all that need be said.

So pretty, Esmerelda is—
So happy and so free!
All day she plays with Chadwick
In the bay, beside the sea.

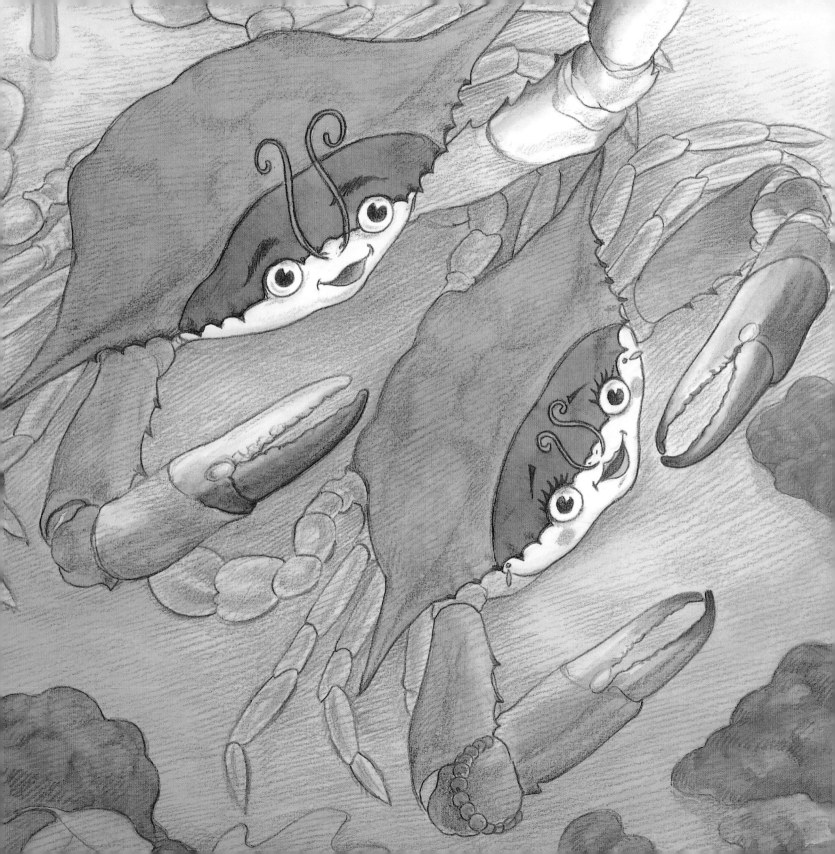

Though Chadwick and his many friends
Are different as can be,
They live together happily
In a bay, beside the sea.

Schiffer Books are available at special discounts for bulk purchases for sales promotions or premiums. Special editions, including personalized covers, corporate imprints, and excerpts can be created in large quantities for special needs. For more information contact the publisher:

Published by Schiffer Publishing Ltd.
4880 Lower Valley Road
Atglen, PA 19310
Phone: (610) 593-1777; Fax: (610) 593-2002
E-mail: Info@schifferbooks.com

For the largest selection of fine reference books on this and related subjects, please visit our website at www. schifferbooks.com
We are always looking for people to write books on new and related subjects. If you have an idea for a book please contact us at the above address.

This book may be purchased from the publisher.
Include $5.00 for shipping.
Please try your bookstore first.
You may write for a free catalog.

In Europe, Schiffer books are distributed by
Bushwood Books
6 Marksbury Ave.
Kew Gardens
Surrey TW9 4JF England
Phone: 44 (0) 20 8392 8585;
Fax: 44 (0) 20 8392 9876
E-mail: info@bushwoodbooks.co.uk
Website: www.bushwoodbooks.co.uk